THE MAN CAVE

A CASE FILES SHORT STORY

RACHEL AMPHLETT

The Man Cave © 2021 by Rachel Amphlett

The moral rights of the author have been asserted.

No part of this book may be reproduced in any form or by any electronic or mechanical means, including information storage and retrieval systems, without written permission from the author, except for the use of brief quotations in a book review.

This is a work of fiction. While the locations in this book are a mixture of real and imagined, the characters are totally fictitious. Any resemblance to actual people living or dead is entirely coincidental.

Forcing open eyelids crusty with sleep and dried tears, Darren raised his chin and choked back the urge to take a deep breath.

A fetid stink clung to the air, one that suggested whatever that smell was, there were sure as hell particles of it hanging around, waiting to creep across his tongue before seeping into his lungs.

An underlying stench of rotten *something* lingered as an undertone to the overall atmosphere.

Perhaps it was vegetables in the dustbin he could see through the cobweb-cracked window near the ceiling.

Perhaps a leftover chicken carcass.

Perhaps not.

He lowered his gaze, a single tear rolling

over his cheek with embarrassment at the stain covering his lap.

His beat-up sneakers had swept scruffy arcs over the debris-strewn and dusty concrete floor, the footprint-shaped grey rainbows a reminder of the hours he'd already spent trying to shuffle out of the hard wooden pine chair he was tied to.

Through the window – a solitary pane maybe eight inches high and a foot wide, and too narrow to squeeze through – weak sunlight teased and danced its way from the horizon.

Shivering, his body craving warmth and clothing more suitable to being held captive than ripped denim jeans and a thin late-eighties Aerosmith T-shirt, he realised the solid weight of his Rolex watch was missing from his wrist.

He gritted his teeth.

On the wall, over to his right, a decades-old central heating system grumbled and shook itself to life, the pipework next to it rattling as it sent warmth up through the ducting system and into the three-bedroom house.

Darren counted the seconds off in his head before the familiar clanging from the air in the system began, and then the pressure reached temperature, pushing warmth into the rooms above.

Morning, then.

Half past six, to be exact.

Plenty of time to plan his revenge.

Whoever had done this, whoever had attacked him, would pay.

It had been nine thirty when the lights had gone out the night before.

Plunged into darkness, he dropped the knife he had been using to gut the trout and clutched at the sides of the kitchen worktop, shocked and disoriented at the sudden transition before glancing at his watch.

The luminous dials had ruined his night vision in the split second it took to register the time.

Stumbling his way past the ceramic sink clogged with grime and gristle, hands held out in front of him, he'd located the keys hanging on an old iron nail next to the back door. He fumbled a cylindrical fob on the ring and twisted it clockwise.

The miniature flashlight was a goofy consolation prize from a fair in Clearfield two years ago when he'd been trying to win a giant teddy bear for Tess. Now the narrow beam provided enough light to guide him to the cellar door.

As he ran his gaze over the fuse box fastened to the wall at the top of the wooden staircase, he'd spotted the trip switch in its off position and reached out to flick it back on.

He frowned while he tried to recall any noise, any warning that preceded the blow to his shoulder that sent him tumbling down the flight, each tread adding bruises to his arms, his legs, his hips.

All he could remember was a blinding flash as the power returned and the lights ignited – and then darkness when the back of his skull met the rough concrete surface of the cellar floor.

Had they tied him up and then ransacked the house, searching for cash, his laptop and more?

Darren clenched his teeth, then ran his tongue over his split lip and squinted as the sun crested the edge of the dusty window sill, ducking his head to the side as a single ray sought him out, blinding him.

Digging his heels into the dust, he heaved the chair away from the light, groaning under the strain, wishing he had listened to his wife and lost those extra pounds around his waist.

Sweat beading at his brow, panting with the effort, he vowed to get in shape the moment he got home. For now, at least he was out of the sun's glare.

That would have to do.

He peered at the window a moment longer, resigned to the acknowledgement that it was too small for his thickset frame to squeeze through, and then turned his head and ran his gaze over two metal filing cabinets that lined the stone wall of the basement to his left.

A workbench stood beside them, its surface wiped clean and free from dust.

The cabinets had been there when his grandfather had been alive, salvaged from a garage sale a couple of miles away then used to collect mismatched nuts and bolts, torn pieces of worn and scratched sandpaper, a fist-sized ball of rubber bands – the detritus of sixty years of saving bits and pieces.

Just in case.

Darren had found his own use for the cabinets over the years since his grandfather's death. He cleared away the rusting history and spent a whole weekend filling bags he then took to the dump on the outskirts of town before he returned and oiled the locks.

Tess had never liked the house, or its remote and wild location beyond the urban sprawl of the city, and refused to visit after the first time she had set eyes on it. She had begged him to sell it every year of their six-year marriage, telling him it gave her the creeps.

He couldn't.

The place held too many memories, too much history to simply discard it like some unwanted object.

Who knew what would become of the place in his absence if he sold up?

Instead, he returned to the house every two months and chipped away at the jobs that needed doing, organising and cataloguing the history that remained.

A shovel and a pickaxe were propped against the far wall. There were tools in two of the filing cabinet drawers, including pliers and saws.

He knew because he prided himself on keeping them in pristine condition, ready to use at a moment's notice. The rugged terrain around the property was treacherous, with ankle-ripping tree roots entangled around granite rocks and boulders that made it impossible to move fast.

Darren kept a routine – every eight weeks, he would carve his way through the undergrowth, carrying the tools and pushing a wooden barrow that had once been used to transport coal between the outbuilding and the house each winter.

Even the barrow propped next to the back door served a different purpose since his grandfather had passed away.

And now the house had been invaded, his memories soiled by whoever had attacked him last night.

Thank God Tess hated the house.

Thank God she hadn't been here when it happened.

Who knew what could have happened to her otherwise?

The thought of strangers traipsing over the oak floorboards, wandering through the gnarled woodland surrounding the house tensed his shoulders. A flare of anger replaced confusion, a renewed determination to escape driven by a need for revenge that burned his gut.

There would be something in those drawers he could use to aid his escape, he was sure.

If only he could get into them.

A chink of sunlight caught the locks, polished and gleaming, teasing.

Where were the keys?

They had been in his hand the night before – before he'd been assaulted, before the lights came back on.

Had he clutched them in his hand as he'd fallen, or had he dropped them at the top of the stairs?

Darren craned his neck, rocking the chair back until he could see up the stairs in the gloom.

No keys taunted him from the thirteen treads leading up to the closed cellar door.

He cursed under his breath and let the chair fall forward with a dull thud, his stomach sinking with the realisation that there would be no easy escape.

As if realising his predicament and determined to taunt him, the trill of his mobile phone ringing upstairs filtered down through the closed door to where he sat lashed to the chair.

He recognised the lame tune he'd finally downloaded earlier in the summer, a rock anthem he and Tess had fallen in love with at college.

The sort of song the car radio got turned up for – loud.

The sort of song they sang together, laughing at the memories it evoked.

Tess—

The phone rang out, and he wondered if it had been her trying to reach him.

At least she was safe.

She'd complained about the four-day software conference out of town, saying they could have had a long weekend away together instead if it wasn't for the job promotion she wanted.

He closed his eyes.

Three more days until she returned to their apartment.

Three days until she discovered he hadn't returned from the house in the woods.

His tongue scratched across the roof of his

mouth and he blinked, attempting to lose the spots that were forming at the periphery of his vision, blurring the edges of his sight. He crunched his eyelids closed. The headache had started again, wrapping its fingers around the base of his skull before crawling over his head and punching him between the eyes.

A clear plastic bottle of water caught his attention, the bright blue screw-on cap visible above the vice clamped to the edge of the workbench.

He licked his lips and tried to remember when he'd placed it there, whether it was full – and if the bottle was full of water, or turpentine or white spirit instead.

No matter – he couldn't reach it from here, unless…

Darren dug his heels into the floor.

First, he shuffled and scraped until he'd turned the chair – from his attempt to find the keys, he'd deduced it was easier travelling backwards rather than forwards while his calves were tied to the wooden legs.

Next, he shoved the chair towards the workbench.

Dig in, shove.

Dig in, shove.

The scrape of wood against concrete bounced off the cinderblock walls and reverberated in his skull, aggravating the headache, making it worse.

Taking deep gulps of air, panting from the effort, he wondered if anyone had heard him, and held his breath for a moment.

Nothing. Just the buzz of flies and the creaking of the window frame as it expanded in the sun's glare.

Dig in, shove.

Dig in, shove.

Gritting his teeth, he reached the first filing cabinet and turned his head, grimacing as half a dozen flies lifted into the air from the locked drawers and buzzed around his nose and mouth.

He shook his head, growling under his breath, then continued his journey past the second filing cabinet. A bloody fingerprint smudged the top drawer's lock and he wondered fleetingly why he hadn't wiped it away.

He paused to catch his breath.

Tess had been nagging him these past two months to join a gym, but he'd never seen the point. He could lift several pounds, he'd argued. He did so every day in his construction job. Why pay to lift weights during his time off?

Not weights, cardio, Tess had said, her lips pursed – and then she'd shaken her head and walked away.

Now, with sweat beading his brow and neck,

dripping between his shoulders, he wondered if he should have listened to her.

He let his head drop forward, the strain in his shoulders burning his muscles while the ropes that bound his wrists behind the chair dug into his skin.

Survival. That's what this was about.

He had to get out of here. Had to find out who had done this.

Dig in, shove.

Dig in, shove.

Now his shoulder was level with the vice clamped to the workbench, the steel surface of the table clear from tools and only an old rag and the water bottle to show for his last venture down here.

Darren jerked his wrists, testing the plastic ties that held him – but they wouldn't yield. Instead, the edges cut into the skin, blood trickling across his palms and over his fingers.

He licked his lips then shuffled closer to the workbench, craning his neck, his mouth apart like a cat fish seeking bait.

Baring his teeth, he lunged for the bottle, biting the blue cap.

It was heavier than he expected. His heart lurched as his mouth took the weight, panic setting in at the thought that it would topple and roll away from him.

He bit down harder and dragged it over the edge of the bench, swiping it away.

The bottle dropped into his lap and rolled forward.

Darren clenched his knees together, tipped the chair back and emitted a cry as the precious water stopped in its tracks.

Lowering his head, he used his teeth to right it between his knees, then paused.

How tight had he screwed the cap back on?

He had a habit of twisting bottle caps tight – and then, as an afterthought, would give it a little extra twist. Paranoia, caused by a bottle of soft drink tipping over in the car one afternoon after a football game and Tess complaining about the sweet stench in the upholstery for weeks afterwards.

His breathing was hollow now, hot and desperate.

Tightening his grip, he chewed the cap between his teeth and twisted.

Nothing – except a dull ache at the base of an incisor that reminded him that his jaw had taken a beating on the way down the cellar steps.

Angrier, in pain, he ran his tongue across his teeth before repositioning them around the bottle cap.

He clenched his thighs, forcing pressure into

his knee joints to grip the bottle, and twisted once more.

It happened so fast, it took him a moment for his brain to process what had gone wrong.

The cap loosened from the bottle with little warning, jerking Darren's head backwards.

Shocked by the sudden movement, he relaxed his legs, the dull *squish* of the plastic bottle bouncing off the concrete floor reaching him a split second after he could react.

"No—"

Too late, he shifted in the chair in time to see the bottle roll under the workbench leaving a trail of precious water to mark its trajectory.

Darren let his head drop forwards, closed his eyes, and cursed.

It couldn't be money. He owed no-one anything – he and Tess paid their bills on time, lived a frugal life, and never borrowed, apart from the mortgage on the apartment.

Blackmail?

There hadn't been any threats, no warnings.

Who knew about the house?

There were no signposts to it back on the road, and the undulating track was almost half a mile long, overgrown and unkempt compared to the back of the property. Deliberately so, designed to keep people away when he wasn't around.

That and the chain across the track a few yards before the house came into view.

Movement next to his right foot pulled him from his thoughts, and he glanced down.

No.

No, no, no.

Beady eyes appraised him, nose twitching as the rat raised itself on its hindquarters. Without warning, it scampered across his feet to the water droplets that dotted the floor and began to lap.

Darren lashed out with his foot, a grunt of satisfaction escaping his mouth as the rodent's body landed with a soft thud against the nearest filing cabinet.

It wasn't dead.

The rat glared at him with a disdain that sent a shiver across his shoulders, then raised its nose to the metal drawers, unperturbed by the flies gathering there.

Darren wasted no time. He dug his heels in and made slow, painful progress back to the cellar steps.

The rat watched him for a moment, then began to clean itself, rubbing tiny paws over its whiskers and nose.

Darren kept his eyes on the rodent and craned his neck until he could see the cellar door and called out.

"Is anyone up there? Hello?"

He clamped shut his mouth, his teeth rattling together.

The walls were thick, thicker than they were when his grandfather died. Reinforced. Sound-proofed with the best quality materials he could find.

He had no idea how the rat had got in, and he didn't care.

Darren choked back the next thought that entered his head.

Was his attacker coming back?

What if he had been left here, abandoned?

Forgotten?

What if something had happened to the person who had shoved him down the stairs?

What if no-one else knew he was here?

Tess was away for three more days, and now he had no water. While she was at that software conference, dining out in five star luxury morning and night, he was here.

Trapped.

Sure, he reckoned he could last without food – but water?

The rat lowered its paws and eyed him, a raw hunger in its eyes.

He smacked dry lips, tried to batten down the panic, and failed.

"Help me!"

The words were out of his mouth before he could stop them. He clamped his mouth shut, shocked by the fear trembling his voice.

Then—

A footfall, above his head as if someone had stepped into the kitchen and paused.

"Hello? Who's there?"

The seconds passed, the silence drawing out until he couldn't bear it any longer.

"Let me out!"

"How are you doing down there, Darren?"

"Tess?" Utter confusion clutched at his chest. "Is that you?"

'Did you have a busy weekend planned?"

His brow creased, his thoughts spinning. "I thought you were away. I thought you weren't coming back until Monday."

A sigh carried through the door.

A sigh that held pain, loathing, disgust.

"I know about the others, Darren."

Her voice was soft, musical.

That made the accusation even worse.

"What others? I've never cheated on you, Tess. That's the truth."

She didn't answer right away, and his breath caught in his throat.

He'd been so careful. All this time, he'd been so careful…

"Let me tell you what I know, Darren. The

first filing cabinet is for purses, watches and cell phones…"

Gritting his teeth, he strained at the plastic ties cutting into his flesh.

How could she know?

How did she find out?

"The second filing cabinet…" Her voice broke, then there was a loud sob before she beat the cellar door with her fist. "How could you?"

He glared across the basement at it now, the flies buzzing at the drawers, headbutting the cool steel surface in vain, the inquisitive rat sniffing at the metal surfaces, seeking a way in.

"That's where you keep everything else, isn't it Darren?"

Yes, the voice in his head screamed.

Everything else.

Everything catalogued.

Everything organised.

"Fingers, Darren," Tess said, her voice little more than a whisper.

He could sense her, trembling at the door while she spoke the words to him, her mouth close to the thick oak surface.

"Lips," she said. "Toes… The rest… I found the graves out in the woods, Darren."

"Wait, Tess. You don't understand. Don't call the police."

She laughed then, a rich guttural burst that exuded bitterness – and something else.

He reared back in shock, the chair tilting on its legs. "Tess?"

"I'm the only one who knows you're here," she said, a menace creeping into her voice, a bitter confidence he hadn't heard before. "No-one knows about the house except me, do they?"

"No…"

It was true. He never invited anyone here. Never mixed with the locals. Kept his distance.

For good reason.

"The police aren't coming," she hissed. "*No one's* coming. You can rot down there, Darren Forbes. You deserve to die a slow death for what you've done."

She thumped the door once before her footsteps retreated from the top of the stairs.

He peered up at the ceiling as she paced across the kitchen, her heels clacking on the wooden floorboards, and then the back door slammed shut.

A car engine roared to life beyond the grimy window before he heard the wheels crackle across the stony ground.

"Tess?"

His gaze dropped from the window to the filing cabinets, to the flies buzzing around the drawers.

He heard their tiny wings beating, heard the scratching and scurrying beside the workbench as the rodent became inquisitive once more, and then its nose appeared, twitching as it sought him out.

Darren threw back his head and screamed. "Tess!"

THE END

ABOUT THE AUTHOR

Rachel Amphlett is a USA Today bestselling author of crime fiction and spy thrillers, many of which have been translated worldwide.

Her novels are available in eBook, print, and audiobook formats from libraries and retailers as well as her website shop.

A keen traveller, Rachel has both Australian and British citizenship.

Find out more about Rachel's books at: www.rachelamphlett.com.

Nowhere to Run

When a series of vicious attacks leaves the local
running community in shock and fear, probationary
detective Kay Hunter is thrust into the middle of a
fraught investigation.

ISBN eBook: 978-1-913498-68-9

ISBN paperback: 978-1-913498-69-6

Blood on Snow

A suburban housewife is found dead in her garden. There is no weapon, no witnesses, and the only set of footprints belong to her cat.

Probationary detective Kay Hunter and her colleagues are convinced it's murder – but how can they find a killer when there are no clues?

ISBN eBook: 978-1-913498-70-2
ISBN paperback: 978-1-913498-71-9

The Reckoning

The newest arrival at a care home for the elderly carries an air of mystery that even an ex-WW2 Resistance fighter can't help trying to solve.

Then matters take a sinister turn…

ISBN eBook: 978-1-913498-70-2
ISBN paperback: 978-1-913498-71-9

The Beachcomber

Staying at a tiny guesthouse in Cornwall after the summer, Julie spends her days combing the beaches, looking for things to collect while hiding from her past. Then a storm breaks, and suddenly she's scared.

Because you never know what might wash up after a storm…

ISBN eBook: 978-1-913498-93-1
ISBN paperback: 978-1-913498-94-8